De Vinne Press

Old faces of Roman and medieval types lately added to the De

Vinne Press

De Vinne Press

Old faces of Roman and medieval types lately added to the De Vinne Press

ISBN/EAN: 9783741189784

Manufactured in Europe, USA, Canada, Australia, Japa

Cover: Foto ©Andreas Hilbeck / pixelio.de

Manufactured and distributed by brebook publishing software
(www.brebook.com)

De Vinne Press

Old faces of Roman and medieval types lately added to the De Vinne Press

INTRODUCTORY.

After many years of neglect plain and bold types are again in favor. The Old-style faces, revived by Whittingham and Pickering, have been followed by the Golden, the Chaucer, and the Troy types of William Morris. The Cushing, the Jenson, the De Vinne, and the De Spira faces —all the productions of American typefounders—are attempts more or less successful to put typography in its old and proper field of unadorned simplicity. Types that imitate the delicacy of copper-plate and the ornamentations of lithography are out of fashion. The printer of to-day is oftenest asked to provide bolder types with firm lines that can be easily read. This pamphlet is intended to show, in a full series of sizes, the new faces of this description that have been added to the stock of the De Vinne Press.

The Cushing has been used as a display letter and as a text type for books and pamphlets. It is preferred for its durability, for it has no sharp serifs and no hair-lines that can be easily blunted or gapped.

The Jenson is a fair reproduction of the face made by Nicholas Jenson in 1471, and soon after adopted by typefounders of all countries as the basis or standard of good form for Roman letter. It is not unlike and will compare favorably with the Golden type of William Morris. Note the close fitting of the letters, the protraction of the thick stroke, the infrequency of hair-lines, and the sturdy simplicity of every character.

The Satanick is a revival of the Round Black-letter, or Round Gothic, in general use as a book text before the production of Jenson's form of Roman. This is the style preferred by William Morris for his best books. For reprints of medieval work it will always be a desirable face.

The Ancient Roman, from a German foundry, here seen in capital letters only, is an attempt to combine the severe simplicity of the Old-style with the more rounded forms and more pleasing proportions of modern cuts. Of all·the large Roman capitals now in use this is the one best fitted for the composition of bold book-titles in the style of the seventeenth century, and for modern titles that show one or more words in red ink.

The Louis XV., from a French foundry, will be found a fit type for the texts of small books, printed in the new fashion of capitals only. These characters enable the printer to give a clearness and readability to print that cannot be had by the use of the ordinary form of Roman capitals.

The Century, made in three sizes only, is a slightly compressed letter, with thickened hair-lines. It is especially useful for double-column pages, poetry, and all work for which it is necessary to get many words in a line, and much matter in a page, without loss of legibility.

The De Vinne Press has many other faces not shown in this specimen: the complete series (6-point to 72-point) of the true Caslon Old-style, the Elzevir Old-style, and the Modernized Old-style, and a great variety of faces of modern cut, as well as Headbands, Tailpieces, Initials and Borders, many of original design, all carefully selected to show the different fashions of typography.

Prelum
Ascensianu.

Cushing. Six-point, leaded.

RICHARD DE BURY, AUTHOR OF PHILOBIBLON.

We not only set before ourselves a service to God in preparing volumes of new books, but we exercise the duties of a holy piety, if we first handle so as not to injure them, then return them to their proper places and commend them to undefiling custody, that they may rejoice in their purity while held in the hand, and repose in security when laid up in their repositories. Truly, next to the vestments and vessels dedicated to the body of the Lord, holy books deserve to be most decorously handled by the clergy, upon which injury is inflicted as often as they presume to touch them with a dirty hand. Wherefore, we hold it expedient to exhort students upon negligencies which can be avoided, but which are wonderfully injurious to books.

In the first place, then, let there be a mature decorum in opening and closing of volumes, that they may neither be unclasped with precipitous haste, nor thrown aside after inspection without being duly closed ; for it is necessary that a book should be much more carefully preserved than a shoe. But school folks are in general perversely educated, and, if not restrained by the rule of their superiors, are puffed up with infinite absurdities ; they act with petulance, swell with presumption, judge of everything with certainty, and are unexperienced in anything.

You will perhaps see a stiff-necked youth, lounging sluggishly in his study, while the frost pinches him in winter time, oppressed with cold, his watery nose drops, nor does he take the trouble to wipe it with his handkerchief till it has moistened the book beneath it with its vile dew. For such a one I would substitute a cobbler's apron in the place of his book. He has a nail like a giant's, perfumed with stinking filth, with which he points out the place of any pleasant subject. He distributes innumerable straws in various places, with the ends in sight, that he may recall by the mark what his memory cannot retain. These straws, which the stomach of the book never digests, and which nobody takes out, at first distend the book from its accustomed closure, and, being carelessly left to oblivion, at last become putrid. He is not ashamed to eat fruit and cheese over an open book, and to transfer his empty cup from side to side upon it ; and because he has not his alms-bag at hand, he leaves the rest of the fragments in his books. He never ceases to chatter with eternal garrulity to his companions ; and while he

Solid.

ON THE PROPER CARE OF BOOKS.

adduces a multitude of reasons void of physical meaning, he waters the book, spread out upon his lap, with the spluttering of his saliva. What is worse, he next reclines with his elbows on the book, and by a short study invites a long nap ; and by way of repairing the wrinkles, he twists back the margins of the leaves, to the no small detriment of the volume. He goes out in the rain, and now flowers make their appearance upon our soil. Then the scholar we are describing, the neglecter, rather than the inspector of books, stuffs his volume with firstling violets, roses, and quadrifolia. He will next apply his wet hands, oozing with sweat, to turning over the volumes, then beat the white parchment all over with his dusty gloves, or hunt over the page, line by line, with his forefinger covered with dirty leather. Then as the flea bites, the holy book is thrown aside, which, however, is scarcely closed in a month, and is so swelled with the dust that has fallen into it, that it will not yield to the efforts of the closer.

But impudent boys are to be specially restrained from meddling with books, who, when they are learning to draw the forms of letters, if copies of the most beautiful books are allowed them, begin to become incongruous annotators, and wherever they perceive the broadest margin about the text, they furnish it with a monstrous alphabet, or their unchastened pen immediately presumes to draw any other frivolous thing whatever that occurs to their imagination. There the Latinist, there the sophist, there every sort of unlearned scribe tries the goodness of his pen, which we have frequently seen to have been most injurious to the fairest volumes, both as to utility and price. There are also certain thieves who enormously dismember books by cutting off the side margins for letter-paper (leaving only the letters or text), or the fly-leaves put in for the preservation of the book, which they take away for various uses and abuses, which sort of sacrilege ought to be prohibited under a threat of anathema.

But it is altogether befitting the decency of a scholar that washing should without fail precede reading, as often as he returns from his meals to study, before his fingers, besmeared with grease, loosen a clasp or turn over the leaf of a book. Let not a crying child admire the drawings in the capital letters, lest he pollute the parchment with his wet fingers, for he instantly touches whatever he sees.

Furthermore, laymen, to whom it matters not whether they look at a book turned wrong side upwards or spread before them in its natural order, are altogether unworthy of any communion with books.

Cushing. Six-point, leaded.

THE STAPLE OF NEWS.

By Ben Jonson.

—

Scene: West End of St. Paul's.

Peni-boy, Cymbal, Fitton, Tho. Barber, Canter.

In troth they are dainty rooms; what place is this?
Cymbal. This is the outer-room, where my clerks sit,
And keep their sides, the Register i' the midst;
The Examiner, he sits private there, within;
And here I have my several rowls and fyles
Of News by the alphabet, and all put up
Under their heads.
    P. jun. But those too subdivided?
    Cym. Into Authenticall and Apocryphall.
    Fitton. Or News of doubtful credit; as Barbers' News.
    Cymb. And Taylors' News, Porters', and Watermens' News.
    Fitt. Whereto beside the *Coranti* and *Gazetti.*
    Cymb. I have the News of the season.
    Fitt. As Vacation news,
Term news, and Christmas-news.
    Cymb. And News o' the Faction.
    Fitt. As the Reformed-news. Protestant news.
    Cymb. And Pontifical-news, of all which several,
The Day-books, Characters, Precedents are kept.
Together with the names of special Friends —
    Fitt. And Men of Correspondence i' the Country —
    Cymb. Yes, of all ranks, of all religions,—
    Fitt. Factors and Agents —
    Cymb. Liegers, that lye out
Through all the shires o' the kingdom.
    P. jun. This is fine!
And bears a brave relation! but what says
Mercurius Brittannicus to this?
    Cymb. O Sir, he gains by 't half in half.
    Fitt. Nay, more.
I'll stand to 't. For, where he was wont to get
In, hungry Captains, obscure Statesmen.
    Cymb. Fellows.
To drink with him in a dark room in a tavern.
And eat a sawsage.
    Fitt. We ha' seen 't.

. . . . .

TO THOMAS NASH.

LET ALL HIS FAULTS SLEEPE WITH HIS MOURNEFUL CHEST,
AND THERE FOREVER WITH HIS ASHES REST.
HIS STYLE WAS WITTY, THOUGH HE HAD SOME GALL—
SOMETHING HE MIGHT HAVE MENDED: SO MAY ALL.
YET THIS I SAY, THAT FOR A MOTHER-WIT
FEW MEN HAVE EVER SEEN THE LIKE OF IT.

                       Obit 1600.

Cushing. Eight-point, leaded.

The Staple of News, continued.

Fitt. And dish out News.
Were 't true or false.
  Cymb. Now all that charge is sav'd
The publick Chronicler.
  Fitt. How do you call him there?
. . . .
  Cymb. Yes, dedicated to him.
  Fitt. Or rather prostituted.
  P. jun. You are right, Sir.
  Cymb. No more shall be abus'd, nor Country Parsons
O' the Inquisition, nor busy Justices
Trouble the peace, and both torment themselves
And their poor ign'rant neighbours with inquiries
After the many and most innocent monsters,
That never came i' th' Counties they were charg'd with.
  P. jun. Why, methinks, Sir, if the honest common people
Will be abus'd, why should not they ha' their pleasure,
In the believing lyes, are made for them;
As you i' th' office, making them yourselves?
  Fitt. O Sir! It is the *printing* we oppose.
  Cymb. We not forbid that any News be made,
But that 't be *printed;* for, when News is printed,
It leaves, Sir, to be News, while 't is but written —
  Fitt. Though it be ne're so false, it runs News still.
  P. jun. See divers men's opinions! unto some
The very *printing* of them makes them News;
That ha' not the heart to believe anything,
But what they see in *print.*
  Fitt. I, that 's an error
Has abus'd many: but we shall reform it,
As many things beside (we have a hope)
Are crept among the popular abuses.
  Cymb. Nor shall the Stationer cheat upon the time,
By buttering over again —

ERRATA. EN RONDEAU.

DANS CE VOLUME OÙ SONT TOUTES LES FABLES,
S'IL S'EST GLISSÉ DES FAUTES PEU NOTABLES,
OU QUI NE SOIENT QUE DE L'IMPRESSION,
MANQUE DE SOIN, ET D'APLICATION,
UN MOT POUR L'AUTRE, ELLES SONT EXCUSABLES.

Cushing.   Eight-point, leaded.

THE MEDICAL WISDOM OF OUR ANCESTORS.

A WAY TO GET WEALTH, CONTAINING SIX PRINCIPAL CREATIONS OR CALLINGS, IN WHICH EVERY GOOD HUSBAND OR HOUSE-WIVE may lawfully imploy themselves. This is the 14th edition, dated 1683, in 4to. One of these "Vocations" is "The English House-wife, containing the inward and outward Vertues which ought to be in a compleat Woman. As her Skill in Physick, Chirurgery, Cookery," &c. nearly in the words of the title already given. This is the 9th edition of that part of the volume.   This work is dedicated to The Right Honourable and most Excellent Lady Frances, Countess Dowager of Exeter.

To make Oyl of Swallows. Take Lavender-cotten, Spike-knot-grass, Ribwort, Balm, Valerian, Rosemary tops, Woodbine tops, Vine strings, French Mallows, the tops of Alecost, Strawberry strings, Tutsan, Plantane, Walnut Tree leaves, the tops of young Beets, Isop, Violet leaves, Sage of Vertue, fine Roman Wormwood, of each of them a handful, Camomile, and red Roses, of each two handfuls, twenty quick Swallows, and beat them together in a mortar, and put to them a quart of Neats-foot oyl, or May butter, and grind them all well together, &c. &c. &c. This Oyl is exceeding soveraign for any broken bones, bones out of joynt, or any pain or grief either in the bones or sinews.

Solid.

To preserve your body from the infection of the Plague, a drink is proposed, made of old ale, Mithridate, &c. of which, every morning fasting, take 5 spoonfuls, and after bite and chaw in your moth the dried root of Angelica, or smell on a nosegay made of the tassell'd end of a ship-rope, and they will surely preserve you from infection.

To take away deafness, take a gray Eel with a white belly, and put her into a sweet earthen pot, quick, and stop the pot very close with an earthen cover, or some such hard substance; then dig a deep hole in a horse-dunghil, and set it therein, and cover it with the dung, and so let it remain for a fortnight, and then take it out, and clear out the oyl which will come of it, and drop it into the imperfect ear, or both, if both be imperfect.

If you would not be drunk, take the powder of Betony and Coleworts mixt together, and eat it every morning fasting, as much as will lye upon a sixpence, and it will preserve a man from drunkenness.

The qualifications of a Cook are thus described: First, she must be cleanly, both in body and garments; she must have a quick eye, a curious nose, a perfect taste, and ready ear; (she must not be butter-fingred, sweet toothed, nor faint hearted) for the first will let every thing fall; the second will consume what it should encrease; and the last will lose time with too much niceness.

If you will roast any venison, after you have washed it, and cleansed all the blood from it, you shall stick it with cloves all over on the outside, and if it be lean, you shall lard it, either with mutton lard, or pork lard, but mutton is the best: then spit it, and rost it by a soaking fire, then take vinegar, bread crums, and some of the gravy which comes from the venison, and boyl them well in a dish; then season it with sugar, cinnamon, ginger and salt, and serve the venison forth upon the sawce when it is rosted enough.

Cushing.   Ten-point, leaded.

McCREERY ON BOOKBINDING.

Embodied thought enjoys a splendid rest
On guardian shelves, in emblem costume drest ;
Like gems that sparkle in the parent mine,
Through crystal mediums the rich coverings shine ;
Morocco flames in scarlet, blue, and green,
Impress'd with burnish'd gold, of dazzling sheen ;
Arms deep emboss'd the owner's state declare,
Test of their worth — their age — and his kind care ;
Embalm'd in russia stands a valued pile
That time impairs not, nor vile worms defile ;
Russia, exhaling from its scented pores
Its saving power to these thrice-valued stores,
In order fair arranged in volumes stand,
Gay with the skill of many a modern hand ;
At the expense of sinew and of bone,
The fine papyrian leaves are firm as stone ;
Here all is square as by masonic rule,
And bright the impression of the burnished tool.
On some the tawny calf a coat bestows,
Where flowers and fillets beauteous forms compose :
Others in pride the virgin vellum wear,
Beaded with gold — as breast of Venus fair ;
On either end the silken head-bands twine,
Wrought by some maid with skilful fingers fine —
The yielding back falls loose, the hinges play,
And the rich page lies open to the day.
Where science traces the unerring line,
In brilliant tints the forms of beauty shine ;
These, in our works, as in a casket laid,
Increase the splendour by their powerful aid.

MEN MAY FYNDE IN OLDE BOKYS
WHO SO THEREIN LOKYS
ACTES WORTHY OF MEMORY,
FULL OF KNOWLEDGE AND MYSTERY.

Cushing.   Ten-point, leaded.

ABOUT THE READING OF BOOKS.

That one should possess no books beyond his power of perusal — that he should buy no faster than as he can read straight through what he has already bought — is a supposition alike preposterous and unreasonable. "Surely you have far more books than you can read," is sometimes the inane remark of the barbarian who gets his books, volume by volume, from some circulating library or reading club, and reads them all through, one after the other, with a dreary dutifulness, that he may be sure that he has got the value of his money.

It is true that there are some books — as Homer, Virgil, Horace, Milton, Shakespeare, and Scott — which every man should read, who has the opportunity — should read, mark, learn, and inwardly digest.   To neglect the opportunity of becoming familiar with them is deliberately to sacrifice the position in the social scale which an ordinary education enables its possessor to reach.   But is one next to read through the sixty and odd folio volumes of the Bollandist Lives of the Saints, and the new edition of the Byzantine historians, and the State Trials, and the Encyclopædia Britannica, and Moreri and the Statutes at large, and the Gentleman's

Solid.

Magazine from the beginning, each separately, and in succession? Such a course of reading would certainly do a good deal towards weakening the mind, if it did not create absolute insanity.

But in all these just named, even in the Statutes at large, and in thousands upon thousands of other books, there is precious honey to be gathered by the literary busy bee, who passes on from flower to flower.   In fact, "a course of reading," as it is sometimes called, is a course of regimen for dwarfing the mind, like the drugs which dog-breeders give to King Charles spaniels to keep them small.   Within the span of life allotted to man there is but a certain number of books that it is practicable to read through, and it is not possible to make a selection that will not, in a manner, wall in the mind from a free expansion over the republic of letters.   The being chained, as it were, to one intellect in the perusal straight on of any large book, is a sort of mental slavery superinducing imbecility.   Even Gibbon's Decline and Fall, luminous and comprehensive as its philosophy is, and rapid and brilliant the narrative, will become deleterious mental food if consumed straight through without variety.   It will be well to relieve it occasionally with a little Boston's Fourfold State, or Hervey's Meditations, or Sturm's Reflections for Every Day.

Cushing.　Twelve-point, leaded.

JOHN HILL BURTON ON BOOKS.

It is difficult, almost impossible, to find the book from which something either valuable or amusing may not be found, if the proper alembic be applied.　I know books that are curious, and even amusing, from their excessive badness.　If you want to find precisely how a thing ought not to be said, you take one of them down, and make it perform the service of the intoxicated Spartan slave. There are some volumes in which, at a chance opening, you are certain to find a mere platitude delivered in the most superb and amazing climax of big words, and others in which you have a like happy facility in finding every proposition stated with its stern forward, as sailors say, or in some other mismanagement of composition.

Solid.

FOX ON THE GOOD OF PRINTING.

And herein we have to beholde the admirable worke of Gods wisdome.　For as the first decay and ruin of the Church before began of rude ignorance and lack of knowledge in teachers; so to restore the Church againe by doctrine and learning, it pleased God to open to man the art of printing, the time whereof was shortly after the burning of John Hus and Hierome.　Printing being opened incontinently ministered unto the Church the instruments and tooles of knowledge and learning, which were good bookes and authors which before lay hid and unknowne.　The science of printing being found, immediately followed the grace of God ; which stirred up good wits aptly to conceive the light of knowledge and of judgment : by which light darknesse began to be espied and ignorance to be detected, truth from error, religion from superstition to be discerned, as is above more largely discoursed.

Cushing. Twelve-point, solid.

THE PROLOGUE OF ROBERT COPLANDE.

The godly vse of prudent wytted men
Cannot absteyne theyr auncyent exercyse:
Recorde of late how besily with his pen
The translator of the sayd treatyse
Hath him indeured, in most goodly wise
Bokes to translate, in volumes large and fayre
From Frenche in prose, of goostly examplayre.

As is the floure of Goddes commaundementes,
A treatyse also called Lucydary,
With two other of the seuen sacramentes,
One of cristen men the ordinary,
The seconde the craft to lyue well and to dye.
With dyuers other to mannes lyfe profytable,
A vertuose vse and ryght commendable.

And now this Boke of Christes Passyon
The which before, in Language was to rude
Seyng the matter to be of grete Compassyon
Hath besyed hym that Vyce for to exclude
In Englysshe clere, with grete Solycitude
Out of Frensshe at Wynkyn de Wordes Instaunce
Dayly descryng of Vertues the Fortheraunce.

Leaded.

MERRIE CONCEITED JESTS
OF GEORGE PEELE, GENTLEMAN, A STUDENT IN OXFORD.

BUY, READ AND JUDGE,
THE PRICE DO NOT GRUDGE.
IT WILL DOE THEE MORE PLEASURE
THAN TWICE SO MUCH TREASURE.

Ancient Roman No. 8.

THIS NEW CUT OF ROMAN CAPITAL LETTERS,
DESIGNED AFTER A CAREFUL STUDY OF EARLY MODELS,
HAS THE FIRM AND STRONG LINES AND OTHER
GOOD FEATURES OF THE OLD-STYLE CHARACTER, WITHOUT A
SERVILE IMITATION OF ITS FAULTS.

Ancient Roman No. 9.

IN THE COMPOSITION OF BOOK TITLES
THIS NEW FACE ENABLES THE PRINTER TO REPRO-
DUCE THE CLEAR AND BOLD EFFECT SO MUCH
ADMIRED IN OLD TITLE-PAGES.

Ancient Roman No. 10.

IN BOOK-MAKING
IT IS AN UNWRITTEN BUT TIME-HONORED LAW
THAT ALL TITLES SHOULD BE SET
IN ROMAN CAPITALS ONLY.

Ancient Roman No. 12—Capital.

TITLES IN BLACK-LETTER, IN SCRIPT, ORNAMENTALS, OR ECCENTRICS ARE NEVER SATISFACTORY TO THE EDUCATED BOOK-LOVER.

Ancient Roman No. 12—Two-line.

SQUARE ANTIQUE LETTERS, ORNAMENTALS, OR FANCY LETTERS OF ANY STYLE, DEGRADE THE TITLE. IN JOB TYPE IT IS NOT A TITLE: IT IS A JOB.

Ancient Roman No. 16.

THE LARGE CAPITALS OF MODERN ROMAN TYPES ARE MUCH

Ancient Roman No. 20.

TOO WEAK AND THIN FOR A BOOK TITLE. TO PRINT IN

Ancient Roman No. 24.

RED INK MAKES THE LINE MORE FEEBLE.

Ancient Roman No. 36.

GRACEFUL

Ancient Roman No. 48.

SUPERB

Ancient Roman No. 60.

ROMAN

Ancient Roman No. 72.

TYPES

Jenson. Eight-point, leaded.

THE ORIGIN OF ROMAN TYPES IN ITALY.

HE Italian scribes of the fifteenth century were famous for their beautiful manuscripts, written in a hand entirely different from the Gothic of the Germans, or the Secretary of the French and Netherlands calligraphers. It was only natural that the first Italian printers, when they set up their press at Subiaco, should form their letters upon the best model of the national scribes. The Cicero de Oratore of 1465 is claimed by some as the first book printed in Roman type, although the characters show that the German artists who printed it had been unable wholly to shake off the traditions of the pointed Gothic school of typography in which they had learned their craft. The type of the Lactantius, and the improved type of the works subsequently printed by Sweynheim and Pannartz at Rome, as well as those of Ulric Hahn, were, in fact, Gothic-Romans; and it was not till Nicholas Jenson, a Frenchman, in 1470, printed his Eusebii Praeparatio at Venice, that the true Roman appeared in Italy, which was destined to become the ruling character in European Typography. Fournier and others have considered that Jenson derived his Roman letter from a mixture of

Solid.

alphabets of various countries; but it is only necessary to compare the Eusebius with the Italian manuscripts of the period, to see that no such elaborate selection of models was necessary or likely. Jenson's font is on a body corresponding to English. The font is round and clear, and differing in fashion only from its future progeny. The capital alphabet consists of twenty-three letters (J, U, and W not being yet in use); the lower-case alphabet is the same except that the u is substituted for the v, and in addition there is a long ſ, and the diphthongs. To complete the font, there are fifteen contractions, six double letters, and three points, the .:? making seventy-three punches in all. Jenson's Roman letter fell after his death into the hands of a firm of which Andrea Torresani was head. Aldus Manutius subsequently associated himself with Torresani, and, becoming his son-in-law and heir, eventually inherited his punches, matrices, and types. The Roman fonts of Aldus were eclipsed by his Italic and Greek, but he cut several fine alphabets. Renouard mentions eight distinct fonts between 1494 and 1558. Roman type was adopted before 1473 by Mentelin of Strasburg, whose beautiful letter placed him in the front rank of the German printers. Gunther Zainer, who settled at Augsburg in 1469, after printing some works in the round Gothic, also adopted, in 1472, the Roman of the Venetian School, fonts of which he is said to have brought direct from Italy. The German name of Antiqua, applied to the Roman character, has generally been supposed to imply a reluctance to admit the claim of Italy to the credit of introducing this style of letter. As, however, the Italians themselves called the letter the Lettera Antiqua tonda, the imputation against Germany is unjust. The French, Dutch, and English called it Roman. The early font had no italic of capitals and minuscules, no arabic figures, no small capitals, no reference marks and but few accents. A complete font of modern Roman type, with its accessory italic and accents, consists of not less than two hundred and twenty characters. The cutting of seventy-three punches was not, as type-founding was then done, a serious expense.

Jenson. Eight-point, double leaded.

PAGANUS SINENSIS.

Quod volo narrare
Et simplicibus verbis : —
In coeptis obscuris
Et dolis protervis
Stat solus Paganus Sinensis ;
Et hoc enarrabo his turbis.

Nomen ei fuit Ah Sin,
Nec possum negare
Ejus mores retulisse,
Quod hoc vult indicare,
Sed ridebat pueriliter — blande —
Ut saepe cogebar notare.

In nona Septembris
Sub aethere aperto
(Sperabamus hunc stultum,
Sed), fraude et furto
Decepit Gulielmum — meipsum—
In modo a quo me averto.

Ludebamus nos chartis,
Et cum nobis ludebat
Paganus qui ludum
Non intelligebat ;
Sed ridebat pueriliter semper,
Ut me, sodalemque tondebat.

Ut charti sunt mixti —
Me pudet narrare —
Sodalisque me anxit
Qui novit celare
In manicis optimas chartas,
Intentus, si posset, fraudare.

Sed longum est dictu
Ut nos Sin elusit,
Ut chartas celavit,
Et omnes confusit ;
Et unam e meis subductam
In mediam palmam profusit.

Intuebar sodalem
Intuentem in me ;
Suspirans surrexit,
"Hoc fiet ? Nonne
Hic perdit nos labor Sinensis ?"
Et tunditur Ah Sin iste.

Tunc solus sodalis
Eum pugnis pectebat,
Et terram ut foliis
Is chartis struebat
Celatis Pagano qui ludum
Non bene hunc intelligebat.

In toga Jacobos
Triginta et plures
Reperimus (si falsum
Me vivum combures) ;
Et in unguibus teretibus ceram,
Quâ semper utuntur hi fures.

Hoc est quare renarro,
Et simplicibus verbis,
In coeptis obscuris
Et dolis protervis,
Sui generis est Ah Sin Paganus,
Et hoc declarabo his turbis.

Jenson.   Ten-point, leaded.

THE EARLY ROMAN CHARACTERS OF FRANCE.

RANCE received printing and the Roman character at the same time, the first work of the Sorbonne press in 1470 being in a handsome Roman
letter about Great Primer in size, with a slight sug-
gestion of Gothic in some of the characters. Gering,
a German himself, and his associates, had learned their art at Basle,
but cut, and probably designed, their own letter on the best avail-
able models. Their font is rudely cast, so that several of their words
appear only half-printed in the impression, and have been finished
by hand. It has been stated erroneously, by several writers, on the
authority of Chevillier, that their font was without capitals. The
font is complete in that respect, and Chevillier's expression, "lettres
capitales," as he himself explains, refers to the initial letters for
which blank spaces were left to be filled in by hand. Besides the
ordinary capital and lower-case alphabets, the font abounds in ab-
breviations. This letter was used in all the works of the Sorbonne
press, but when Gering left the Sorbonne and established himself at

Solid.

the Soleil d'Or, in 1473, he made use of a Gothic letter. In his later
works, however, new and greatly improved fonts of the Roman
appear. Jodocus Badius, who by some is erroneously supposed to
have been the first who brought the Roman letters from Italy to
France, did not establish his famous Prelum Ascensianum in Paris
till about 1500, when he printed in Roman types — not, however,
before one or two other French printers had already distinguished
themselves in the introduction of printing from the adopted Roman
characters. The French quickly recognized the opportunities of
printing, but were slow in improving the shapes of the Roman
letter. The improvements subsequently made are largely due to
Geoffrey Tory, who had qualified himself for this work by residence and study in Italy. In 1529 he published "Champ Fleury,
auquel est contenu Lart et Science de la deue et vraye Proportion
des Lettres Attiques quon dit outrement Lettres Antiques, et vul-
gairment Lettres Romaines, proportionees selon le Corps et visage
humain."

Jenson. Ten-point, leaded.

SKELTON ON BOOK-BINDING.

With that of the boke lozende were the claspes,
The margin was illumined al with golden railes,
And bice empictured with grass-oppes and waspes,
With butterflies, and fresh pecocke tails,
Englored with flowers, and slyme snayles,
Envyved pictures well-touched and quickly,
It would have made a man hole that had be right sickly,
To behold how it was garnished and bound,
Encoverde over with gold and tissue fine,
The claspes and bullions were worth a M pounde,
With balassis and carbuncles the border did shine,
With *aurum mosaicum* every other line.

EPITAPH ON GEORGE FAULKNER,
ALDERMAN AND PRINTER OF THE CITY OF DUBLIN.

Turn, gentle stranger, and this urn revere,
O'er which Hibernia saddens with a tear;
Here sleeps George Faulkner, printer, once so dear
To humorous Swift and Chesterfield's gay peer;
So dear to his wronged country and her laws;
So dauntless when imprisoned in her cause;
No alderman e'er graced a weightier board,
No wit e'er joked more freely with a lord.
None could with him in anecdotes confer —
A perfect annual book in Elzevir.
Whate'er of glory life's first sheets presage,
Whate'er the splendour of the title-page;
Leaf after leaf, though learned lore ensues
Close as thy types, and various as thy news;
Yet, George, we see one lot await them all,
Gigantic folios, or octavos small:
One universal finis claims his rank,
And every volume closes in a blank.

Jenson. Twelve-point, leaded.

ROMAN FIRST USED IN THE NETHERLANDS.

 OMAN was introduced into the Nether-
lands by Johannes de Westfalia, who,
it is said, brought it from Italy in the
year 1472. He located at Louvain, and
after a number of works in Semi-gothic,
published in 1483 an edition of Aeneas
Silvius in the Italian letter. His font is elegant, and of
rather a lighter face than most of the early Roman fonts
of other countries. This printer appears to have been the
only one in the Low Countries who used this type during
the fifteenth century; nor was it till Plantin, in 1555, estab-

Solid.

lished his famous press at Antwerp, that the Roman attained
to any degree of excellence. But Plantin, and after him
the Elzevirs, were destined to eclipse all other artists in
their execution of this letter, which in their hands became
a model for the typography of all civilization. It should be
mentioned, however, that the Elzevirs are not supposed to
have cut their own punches. They were printers and not
designers of letters. They had their types made for them
by the best punch-cutters of Holland and of France. The
Roman types which they made famous, and which are
known by their name, are supposed to have been cut by
Christopher Van Dijk, the form of whose letter was subsequently adopted by English printers with only a few im-
material changes. The reputation of Van Dijk as a master
in letter-design was not confined to the typefounding trade.
For designing the lettering upon an inscription in the Stadt
Huys of Amsterdam, he was paid seventy pounds—a large
sum in that time of low prices. ✤ ✤ ✤ ✤ ✤ ✤ ✤ ✤ ✤ ✤

Jenson.   Twelve-point, leaded.

PROCRASTINATION.

Stay, stay the present instant!
Imprint the marks of wisdom on its wings.
O, let it not elude thy grasp, but like
The good old patriarch on record,
Hold the fleet angel fast until he bless thee.

Lose this day loitering, 'twill be the same story
To-morrow, and the next more dilatory.
The indecision brings its own delays,
And days are lost, lamenting o'er lost days.
Are you in earnest? Seize this very minute!
What you can do, or think you can, begin it.
Boldness has genius, power and magic in it.
Only engage, and then the mind grows heated:
Begin it, and the work will be completed.

Think that To-day shall never dawn again.

WITZERLAND distinguished itself by the Roman letter of Amerbach of Basle, and still more so by the beautiful fonts used by Froben of the same city, who, between 1491 and 1527, printed some of the finest books then known in Europe. His Roman was very bold and regular. Christopher Froschouer of Zurich, about 1545, made use of a peculiar and not unpicturesque form of the Roman letter, in which the round sorts were thickened diagonally.

FIRST INTRODUCTION IN ENGLAND.

HE Roman was first introduced in England by Richard Pynson in 1518. This printer's Norman birth, and his close relationship with the typographers of Rouen, as well as his supposed intimacy with the famous Basle typographer Froben, make it highly probable that he procured his letter abroad, or modelled it on that of some of the celebrated foreign printers of his day. The font, though neat and bold in appearance, displays considerable irregularity in the casting, and contains many contractions.

Jenson. Fourteen-point, double leaded.

BRAHMA.

By RALPH WALDO EMERSON.

If the red slayer think he slays,
  Or if the slain think he is slain,
They know not well the subtle ways
  I keep, and pass, and turn again.

Far or forgot to me is near;
  Shadow and sunlight are the same;
The vanished gods to me appear;
  And one to me are shame and fame.

They reckon ill who leave me out;
  When me they fly, I am the wings;
I am the doubter and the doubt,
  And I the hymn the Brahmin sings.

The strong gods pine for my abode,
  And pine in vain the sacred Seven;
But thou, meek lover of the good!
  Find me, and turn thy back on heaven.

HILE Claude Garamond in France was carrying out into noble practice the theories of the form and proportion of letters set out by his master, Geofroy Tory; while the Estiennes at Paris, Sebastian Gryphe at Lyons, Froben at Basle, Froschouer at Zurich, and Christopher Plantin at Antwerp, were refining their alphabets into

models which were to become classical English printers achieved nothing with the Roman type that was not retrograde. For a time a struggle appears to have existed between the Black-letter and the Roman for the mastery of the English press, and at one period the curious spectacle was presented of mixed fonts of each. Always impressionable and unoriginal, the English printer selected the Dutch for his pattern, and vainly tried to imitate Plantin.

THE first English Bible printed in Roman type was the Bassendyne edition of Edinburgh, in 1576. On the authority of Watson we have it that, from the earliest days of Scotch typography, a steady trade in type and labor was maintained between Holland and Scotland. Watson exhibited in his specimen pages the Dutch Romans which at that day were recognized as the most approved letters in use in his country. Utilitarian motives brought one important departure from the first models of the old Roman letter.

Jenson. Thirty-point, solid.

The first part of the seventeenth century saw the creation abroad of various small faces of Roman, foremost among which were those of the beautiful little Sedan editions of Jannon, which gave their name to the body of the microscopic letter in which they were printed. Van Dijk cut a very small type for the Dutch in Black-letter, and afterwards in Roman, which Luce of Paris tried to copy.

Jenson. Thirty-six-point, solid.

There were English ty-
pographers of the 17th
century who had merit.
PRINTING TYPES

Forty-two-point, solid.

Roycroft is distin-
guished for a hand-
some Roman that
he used in his work
TYPOGRAPHY

Jenson. Forty-eight-point.

Caslon face was
ELZEVIRIAN

Fifty-four-point.

Printing of the
FIRST BIBLE

Sixty-point.

Fine Printing
FRANKLIN

Satanick. Six-point, leaded.

Ancient Bookbinding.

OOKBINDING, as an elaborate art, made great progress in the age of Charlemagne. It became more and more the fashion to employ Italian artists and designers. A large collection of richly illustrated manuscripts, ornamented in the most skilful way, is described in the will of a Count Errard, the son-in-law of Louis le Debonnair; but unfortunately not a single volume of his splendid library has been preserved. This is the more to be regretted as a comparison of these bindings, which were so largely due to Italian workmen, might have assisted us in forming a more accurate idea of the progress of art in the ninth century. From the early French chroniclers, too, we hear of many holy books brought by Childebert from Spain, which, had any examples of them reached us, would have shown the style of silver work in the Merovingian age. Unhappily we have no description of these books, the chronicler contenting himself with a description of the gold caskets which held them. Gold and silver were also largely employed in the ornamentation of the rich clasps, with their buttons. Nails of the same material were scattered in the leather which formed the actual bindings, and where wooden covers were used, elaborate carvings were resorted to. A very ancient specimen of binding is preserved in the Cathedral of Monza. It forms the cover to a copy of the Gospels which was presented at the beginning of the seventh century, by Theodolind, Queen of the Lombards, to the Basilica. It is composed of gold plates, but has a cross set with precious stones in the centre, and several cameos, two of which are restorations of the year 1773. The cover bears a Latin inscription to the effect that "Of the gifts which

Solid.

God has given her, the glorious Queen Theodolind offers this book to St. John the Baptist in the Basilica founded by her at Monza, near the Palace." Labarte gives a facsimile of this binding, as well as of that which belonged to Charles the Bald. The British Museum contains a copy of the Latin Gospels with binding of the eighth or ninth century. It is a beautiful specimen, and it is supposed that the entire work belongs to one period. The plates which cover the boards are of silver. The centre contains the figure of a saint in high relief, one hand raised, the other holding a book. The book in the saint's hand, which has clasps, is ornamented with a geometrical pattern over the whole of its surface. The raised border of the covers is very massive, and is also composed of silver plates, in which large uncut crystals and precious gems are set, and which stand out very prominently. The corners of this valuable book have square medallions of gold with black enamels, representing emblems of the four Evangelists. Another volume of the tenth century has rich blue enamelling, with large crystals set in the bordering. In the Libri collection we read of a Lectionarium which is thus described: "Manuscript upon vellum, of the eleventh or twelfth century, in an ornamented cover, forming a diptych, both sides being gilt and silvered metal, with ivory carvings, figures in alto-relievo, and enamels in taille d'épargne." The book contains thirty-two large ivory medallions (sixteen on each side), representing the old prophets and saints with their symbols, and having inscriptions in ancient uncial letters, the whole surrounded with a foliage of ivory work in the Greek style, with a bead ornament, carved in compartments. The ivory medallions are very early, probably as old as the sixth century, whilst the enamel and metal ornamentations are specimens of handiwork of a later period. To make room for the metal work, the old ivory borders have been slightly cut into, and for the same purpose one of the arms of the crucifix has been shortened. This Lectionarium has evidently been inserted in its present cover at a later period, the original one having most probably been damaged or destroyed by use. We find that in the early part of the Middle Ages the richest materials were employed in the bindings of books. In the Cluny Museum two magnificent plates of Limoges enamel are preserved, which evidently formed part of the cover of a book. On some especially valued writings, as on a Book of Prayers belonging to Philip the Bold, Duke of Burgundy, pearls, gold nails and rubies were lavishly sown, and there is an account of a copy of Boccaccio which was "covered with red velvet, and on each cover five large rubies." It thus became necessary to provide an every-day dress for volumes which were so expensively decorated. After the goldsmith had finished his work, it was returned to the bookbinder, who placed over its rich cover a more ordinary wrapper which served to protect it from injury. ✎ ✎ ✎ ✎ ✎ ✎ ✎ ✎ ✎ ✎ ✎ ✎ ✎

Satanick. Six-point, leaded.

Henry Stephens on Bookselling, 1569.

I am harass'd by the crowd of those
At Frankfort — who their wares expose;
And ever ask'd: "What are you doing,
"In prospect of the fair ensuing?
"New works you'll shew — impressions splendid,
"Where Learning stands by Art commended."
If I say "No;"—"'Tis strange! what none?
"At least then promise—next but one."
Still say I "No;" expostulation
Assumes the tone of indignation:
That Frankfort mart's so strangely slighted;
And broke the faith — I never plighted.
Again these quidnuncs set aside,
With letters, ceaseless, I'm annoy'd;
Italian, English, German, French,
All on my studious hours entrench:
"What last has been achiev'd, and ended?
"What are the impressions next intended?"
Nor to such modest queries stinted,
Of books in print, or to be printed —
A thousand others they propound,
Which even a prophet would confound.
But still, our German billets doux
The interminable theme renew;
Remind me of the fair — the fair —
And hold me constant debtor there.

Of what advantage all these letters?
Not stimulants they are, but fetters.
As though you'd spur a steed that's idle,
Yet check his progress with the bridle.
My press resents the condescension,
That to such foppery gives attention:
Stands still, and bids them longer stay for
All they suggest, desire, and pray for.

For this annoyance then — be sure
Not small — intent to find a cure,
Of books to former fairs I've given,
Or now project, by leave of heaven,
These pages few, as best may suit you,
In form of "Catalogue" salute you:
Which you'll my " Rescript " please to call,
Addrest to none and yet to all.
Thus, " Walls I whiten " — " two," sirs? tush —
A thousand— " with a single brush."

Of works imprest, or held in view
To imprint, deem you the number few?
Reflect — the custom of the fair
Deals not alike with every ware;
But reckons some by count or tale.
Whilst weight of others rules the sale.

Satanick.   Eight-point, leaded.

Bookbinding after the Invention of Printing. The Fifteenth and Sixteenth Centuries.

HE discovery of printing entirely changed the character of bookbinding. The general use, for binding, of calf and morocco — the latter introduced by the Venetians from the East — seems to have followed closely upon the production of the works of Gutenberg and Fust, in 1450. There are many printed books, still in good preservation, that were bound in calf with oaken boards at the end of the fifteenth century. The introduction of paper made from rags, which took the place of parchment, led to the employment of parchment for the bindings of more ordinary books, and there is no question that much valuable literature was lost in the application of old parchment manuscripts to binding purposes. Many of the manuscripts in the Clermont Library were bought by Father Sirmond for fifty écus from a Lorraine bookbinder, who was going to use them to re-cover his volumes. Agobard's writings on the Theology of the ninth century were rescued in much the same way. In a book that is too little known ("Recherches historiques et remarquables," 1713), we read that "Masson, being in the Rue Mercière in Lyons, discovered the works of Agobard, which a bookbinder

Solid.

was about to tear up to bind some volumes. Masson purchased the manuscript, which may yet be seen in the King's Library." In the fifteenth century, Books of Prayers were often bound with a leather covering, which extended beyond the margin of the boards; this was gathered into a knot at the end, by which the volume could be hung at the girdle. As books multiplied, their money-value became less; cheapness and utility began to be regarded in binding them, and it was only in great libraries and monasteries that elaborate bookbindings were continued. As a rule, boards, clasps, and nails were laid aside, silken and woolen fabrics but seldom adopted, and leather and parchment were in ordinary use. Libraries were often kept in towers for quiet and seclusion. The books were arranged on shelves, with the edges outside. In "Noontide Leisure" we have an account of a room which Shakspere called his own, which was fitted up in the Gothic style, well stored with books, of which the leaves, not the backs, were placed in front, and these were decorated with silver strings, and occasionally with gold and silver clasps, in order to confine the sides of the cover. Bishop Earle, in his "Microcosmographie," speaking of a scholar at the university, says, "His study has commonly handsome shelves, and books with neat silk strings, which he shows to his father's man, and is loth to untie or take down for fear of misplacing." As a rule, it must have been very difficult to find any book that was needed on the library shelves, for the titles were rarely visible, only being sometimes written in large letters across the edges of the leaves; more usually they were upon one side of the leather cover. Sometimes, however, we meet with parchment-covered volumes in which the vellum overlapped the edges, and the title was written on the flap. ❧ ❧ ❧ ❧ ❧ ❧ ❧ ❧ ❧ ❧ ❧ ❧

Satanick.   Eight-point, leaded.

from the Ship of fools, 1509.

That in this ship the chiefe place I governe,
By this wide sea with foolis wandering,
The cause is plaine and easy to discerne;
Still am I busy bookes assembling,
for to have plentie is a pleasaunt thing,
In my conceyt, to have them ay in hand,
But what they meane do I not understande.

But yet I have them in great reverence
And honour, saving them from filth and ordure;
By often brusshing and much diligence,
full goodly bounde in pleasaunt coverture
Of damas, sattin, or els of velvet pure:
I keepe them sure, fearing least they should be lost,
for in them is the cunning wherein I me boast.

. . . .

Lo in likewise of bookes, I have store,
But few I reade, and fewer understande;
I folowe not their doctrine, nor their lore,
It is enough to beare a booke in hande:
It were too much to be in such a lande;
for to be bounde to loke within the boke
I am content on the fayre coveryng to looke.

Each is not lettred that nowe is made a lorde,
Nor eche a clerke that heth a benefice;
They are not all lawyers that plees do recorde,
All that are promoted are not fully wise;
On such chance now fortune throwes her dice:
That though one knowe but the yrish game
Yet would he have a gentleman's name.

So in likewise, I am in such a case,
Though I nought can, I would be called wise;
Also I may set another in my place
Which may for me my bookes exercise;
Or els I will ensue the common guise,
And say concedo to every argument,
Lest by much speech my Latin should be spent.

30

Theo. L. De Vinne & Co.

Satanick. Ten-point, leaded.

Of the Craft of Poynting.

"THEREBE fiue maner pontys, and diuisions most
vside with cunnying men: the which, if they be
wel vsid, make the sentens very light, and esy to
vnderstond both to the reder, & the herer, &
they be these: virgil, come, parentheses, playnt
poynt, and interrogatif. A virgil is a selender stryke: lenynge
fyrwarde thiswyse, be tokynynge a lytyl, short rest without
any perfetnes yet of sentens: as betwene the fiue poyntis a fore
rehersid. A come is with tway titils thiswyse: betokynyng a
longer rest: and the sentens yet ether is vnperfet: or els, if it
be perfet: ther cummith more after, longyng to it: the which
more comynly can not be perfet by itself without at the lest
summat of it: that gothe a fore. A parenthesis is with tway
crokyd virgils: as an olde mone, & a new bely to bely: the
whiche be set on theton afore the begynyng, and thetother after

Solid.

the latyr ende of a clause: comyng within an other clause: that
may be perfet: thof the clause, so comyng betwene: wer awey
and therefore it is sowndyde comynly a note lower, than the
vtter clause. yf the sentens cannot be perfet without the ynner
clause, then stede of the first crokyde virgil a streght virgil wol
do very wel: and stede of the later must nedis be a come. A
playne point is with won titill thiswyse. & it cumeth after
the ende of al the whole sentens betokynyng a longe rest. An
interrogatif is with tway titils; the vpper rysyng this wyse?
& it cumeth after the ende of a whole reason: whereyn ther
is sum question axside. the whiche ende of the reson, tri-
yng as it were for an answare: risyth upwarde. we haue
made these rulis in englisshe: by cause they be as profitable, and
necessary to be kepte in euery mother tunge, as in latin. Sethyn
we (as we wolde be god: euery precher wolde do) haue kept
owre rulis bothe in owre englisshe, and latyn: what nede we,
sethyn owre own be sufficient vnough: to put any other exem-
plis." ⚜ ⚜ ⚜ ⚜ ⚜ ⚜ ⚜ ⚜ ⚜ ⚜ ⚜ ⚜ ⚜ ⚜ ⚜ ⚜ ⚜ ⚜

Satanick.   Ten-point, leaded.

The Aldine Anchor.
An Impromptu.

"Let your emblems, or devices, be a dove, or a fish, or a
musical lyre, or a naval anchor."

Would you still be safely landed,
  On the Aldine anchor ride.
Never yet was vessel stranded
  With the dolphin by its side.

Fleet is Wechel's flying courser,
  A bold and brideless steed is he;
But when winds are piping hoarser,
  The dolphin rides the stormy sea.

Stephens was a noble printer,
  Of knowledge firm he fixt his tree;
But time in him made many a splinter,
  As, old Elzevir, in thee.

Whose name the bold Digamma hallows,
  Knows how well his page it decks;
But black it looks as any gallows
  Fitted for poor authors' necks.

Nor time nor envy e'er shall canker,
  The sign that is my lasting pride.
Joy, then, to the Aldine anchor,
  And the dolphin at its side.

To the dolphin, as we're drinking,
  Life, and health, and joy we send;
A poet once he saved from sinking,
  And still he lives — the poet's friend.

Satanick. Twelve-point, leaded.

The Old and the New.

OR artes are like to okes, which by little and little, grow a long time, afore they come to their full bigness. That one man beginneth, another oft times furthereth and mendeth; and yet more praise to be given to the beginner, than to the furtherer or mender, if the first did find more good things than the follower did adde. Experience teacheth that each thing which is invented by man hath a beginning, hath an increase, and hath also in time a full riepness. Now, although each worke is most commendable when

Solid.

it is brought to his full perfection, yet, where the workmen are many, there is oftimes more praise to be given to him that beginneth a good work, than to him that endeth it. For if ye consider the bookes that are now printed, and compare them with the bookes that were printed at the first, Lord, what a diversity is there, and how much do the last exceed the first! Yet if you will compare the first and the last printer together, and seek whether deserveth more praise and commendation, ye shall find that the first did farre exceede the last: for the last had help of manye, and the first had help of none. So that the first lighteth the candle of knowledge (as it were), and the second doth but snuff it. 🙢 🙢 🙢 🙢 🙢 🙢 🙢 🙢 🙢 🙢 🙢 🙢

"The Art of Reason," by Raphe Lever, 1573.

Satanick.   Twelve-point, leaded.

The Poet's Pen.

I was an useless reed; no cluster hung
My brow with purple grapes, no blossom flung
The coronet of crimson on my stem;
No apple blushed upon me, nor (the gem
Of flowers) the violet strewed the yellow heath
Around my feet, nor jessamine's sweet wreath
Robed me in silver: day and night I pined
On the lone moor, and shiver'd in the wind.
At length a poet found me.   From my side
He smoothed the pale and withered leaves, and dyed
My lips in Helicon.   From that high hour
I spoke! My words were flame and living power.
All the wide wonders of the earth were mine,
Far as the surges roll, or sunbeams shine;
Deep as earth's bosom hides the emerald;
High as the hills with thunder clouds are pall'd.
And there was sweetness round me, that the dew
Had never wet so sweet on violets blue.
To me the mighty sceptre was a wand,
The roar of nations peal'd at my command;
To me the dungeon, sword, and scourge were vain;
I smote the smiter, and I broke the chain;
Or tow'ring o'er them all, without a plume,
I pierced the purple air, the tempest's gloom,
Till blaz'd th' Olympian glories on my eye,
Stars, temples, thrones, and Gods — infinity.

Luigi Pulci.

ῌAT a man can write
out clearly, correctly,
and briefly, without
book or reference of
any kind, that he un-
doubtedly knows, whatever else he may
be ignorant of. For knowledge that
falls short of that—knowledge that is
vague, hazy, indistinct, and uncertain—I

Solid.

for one profess no respect at all.   And
I believe that there never was a time or
country where the influences of careful
training were in that respect more
needed. Men live in haste, write in
haste—I was going to say think in
haste, only that perhaps the word thinking is hardly applicable to that large
number who, for the most part, purchase
their daily allowance of thought ready
made.

Lord Stanley.

Satanick. Twenty-four-point, leaded.

 HIS man, suddenly, and without any thought of the work to be done, says to himself: "I mean to write a book," without any other call for writing than his need for fifty pistoles. It is of no use for me to say: "Take a saw, Dioscorus: saw, turn a lathe, or make wheel-hubs, and you will earn wages. Be a copyist then and transcribe, become a proof-reader in some printing house, but don't write."

La Bruyère, Les Caractères, ch. xv.

Gabriel Naudé, in his curious Addition to the History of Louis XI., page 307, says that even as early as the year 1474, all standard books had been printed in at least one edition and several in three or four editions, all by different printers. Santander writes that more than 15,000 distinct editions were printed before the year 1500.

Satanick.   Thirty-six-point, solid.

french founders at a later day compressed the original Roman.

ARTISTIC TYPE

Forty-two-point, solid.

The art of printing was begun in the City of Paris in the year 1470.

RARE BOOKS.

Satanick. Forty-eight-point, solid.

Bad workmen usually blame their tools. ❀

MAGAZINE

Fifty-four-point, solid.

The Art Preservative of

ALL ARTS

Satanick.   Sixty-point.

Black Letter

NEW ART

Seventy-two-point.

Ex-Libris

BINDER

Louis XV.   Body 5.

Inscription upon the Whittingham Tablet
in the Old Church at Chiswick.

IN A VAULT UNDER THIS CHURCH
LIES THE BODY OF
CHARLES WHITTINGHAM,
LATE OF THIS PARISH, PRINTER,
WHO ATTAINED CONSIDERABLE
EMINENCE IN HIS ART,
PARTICULARLY IN THE PRINTING OF
WOOD ENGRAVING.
HE WAS BORN AT CALLEDON,
IN THE COUNTY OF WARWICK,
16TH JUNE, 1767,
AND DIED AT CHISWICK, 15TH JANUARY, 1840,
AGED 73 YEARS.
IN THE SAME VAULT LIES BURIED
MARY, WIFE OF THE ABOVE;
ALSO
REBECCA WHITTINGHAM, HIS SISTER.

Louis XV.   Body 6.

Among the papers of Benjamin Franklin found after his death was
the following Epitaph written by him when a young man.

THE BODY
OF
BENJAMIN FRANKLIN,
PRINTER,
(LIKE THE COVER OF AN OLD BOOK, ITS CONTENTS TORN OUT,
AND STRIPT OF ITS LETTERING AND GILDING)
LIES HERE FOOD FOR WORMS;
YET THE WORK ITSELF SHALL NOT BE LOST,
FOR IT WILL (AS HE BELIEVED) APPEAR ONCE MORE
IN A NEW AND MORE BEAUTIFUL EDITION,
CORRECTED AND AMENDED BY
THE AUTHOR.

Louis XV. Body 7.

William Budaeus, "the prodigy of France," died August 23, 1540. He gave strict orders that his funeral should be celebrated without pomp. The observance of this charge was the occasion of the following epigram in the form of questions and answers by Melin de St. Gelais:

Q. WHOM NOW EXTINCT DO COUNTLESS FOLLOWERS MOURN?

A. ALAS! BUDÆUS, ON THE BIER EXTENDED.

Q. WHY ARE THE FANE'S KNELL-WAFTING SOUNDS FORBORNE?

A. ON WIDER FLIGHTS HIS FAIR FAME IS SUSPENDED.

Q. ON TORCHES WHY NO LIBERAL SUMS EXPENDED,
AS CUSTOM BIDS, AND HOLY FUNERAL RITE?

A. 'T IS BY THE SOLEMN VEIL OF NIGHT INTENDED
TO MARK THE EXTINCTION SAD OF GALLIA'S LIGHT.

Louis XV. Body 8.

This epitaph is attributed to John Dennis.

NEAR THIS PLACE LIES INTERRED
THE BODY OF MR. SAMUEL BUTLER,
AUTHOR OF HUDIBRAS.
HE WAS A WHOLE SPECIES OF POETS IN ONE!
ADMIRABLE IN A MANNER
IN WHICH NO ONE ELSE HAS BEEN TOLERABLE;
A MANNER WHICH BEGAN AND ENDED IN HIM;
IN WHICH HE KNEW NO GUIDE,
AND HAS FOUND NO FOLLOWERS.

Century Roman. Eight-point, leaded.

ENGLISH BOOKBINDING IN THE SIXTEENTH CENTURY.

The first Englishman who did work in bookbinding that could at all compare with that produced abroad was John Reynes, bookseller and binder to Henry VII. and Henry VIII. He resided at the «George,» in St. Paul's Churchyard, and was an artist of some mark. His devices consisted of two small shields, with his initials and monogram, and these he usually introduced in a large design. Several of his bindings are to be seen in the British Museum. In a show-case in the Manuscript Department is a good specimen, in stamped leather, with an ancient ivory of the Crucifixion (fourteenth century work) let into the upper cover. The leather and pattern are very roughly cut into for the purpose. The volume has Reynes's monogram on the side, and a very elaborate back. M. Libri, in a note to his Catalogue, remarks:—« In some of the most elaborate of Henry VIII.'s blind-tooled books, the instruments of the Passion are accompanied with the inscription, ‹ *Redemptoris mundi arma*,› a curious application of heraldry to the bibliopegistic art by the king's binder, John Reynes, to whom this device is attributed by Ames.» Other binders of this period whose names have come down to us, are Michael Lobley, William Hill, and John Toye. Thomas Berthelet, the king's printer, also bound largely the books he sold to Henry VIII. Most of the work done for Henry VII. and his son was in blind-tooling, of a bold and effective character, but with little pretension to good art. In the twenty-fifth year of Henry VIII. (1533), an Act of Parliament was passed, in the interest

Solid.

of English bookbinders, which was not repealed until the twelfth of George II., by which it was enacted: « That no persones, recyant or inhabytaunt within this Realme, after the seid feast of Christemas next comyng, shal bye to sell agayn any prynted bokes brought frome any partes out of the Kynges obeysance, redy bounden in bourds, lether, or perchement, uppon payne to lose and forfett, for every boke bounde out of the seid Kynges obeysance, and brought into this Realme and bought by any person or persons within the same to sell agayne, contrary to this Act, vjs. viijd.» In the reign of Edward VI., Grolier patterns were introduced into England, and became very popular. The specimens that have come down to us are chiefly of an elaborate and very artistic character. It is a question still undecided whether this work was done by Englishmen, or whether foreigners were brought over to supply materials for the refined taste of the upper classes. The British Museum has a copy of *Xenophon*, that belonged to Edward VI., which is probably of French workmanship. It is ornamented with Tudor roses, and the effect is very fine. In the same Museum is a very elaborate binding of a book that once belonged to Queen Mary I. It is in Gothic style, with painted leather, and painted arms in the centre of the side. A reference to the Household and Wardrobe accounts of the time shows that considerable sums were paid for the binding of these books, but the names of the binders are seldom or never given. An attempt has been made to associate one choice piece of binding with the name of an eminent printer. In the British Museum is the presentation copy, from Fox, the martyrologist, to Queen Elizabeth, of *The Gospels of the Fower Evangelists. Printed by John Daye*, 1571. It is bound in brown calf, with a centre block, and corners inlaid with white kid or morocco. The royal Arms and E. R. are tooled on the calf, which is also beautifully studded with gold.

Century Roman. Eight-point, leaded.

A CONTEMPLATION

ON THE MYSTERY OF MAN'S REGENERATION, IN ALLUSION TO THE
MYSTERY OF PRINTING.

Great blest *Master Printer*, come
Into thy *composing room:*
Wipe away our foul offences,
Make, O make our souls and senses
The *upper* and the *lower cases;*
And thy large alphabet of graces
The *letter*, which being ever fit,
O haste thou to *distribute* it:
For there is (I make amount)
No *imperfection* in the *fount*.
If any letter's face be *foul*,
O wash it ere it touch the soul;
Contrition be the *brush*, the *lye*
Tears from a penitential eye.

Thy graces so *distributed*,
Think not thy work half finished:
On still, O Lord, no time defer,
Be truly a COMPOSITOR;
Take thy *composing stick* in hand,
Thy holy word, the firmest band;
For sure that work can never miss,
That's truly *justified* in this.

The end of grace's distribution,
Is not a mere dissolution;
But that from each part being cited,
They may be again united.
Let righteousness and peace then meet,
Mercy and truth each other greet;
Let these letters make a word,
Let these words a line afford,
Then of lines a page compose,
Which being brought unto a close,
Be thou the *direction*, Lord;
Let love be the fast-binding *cord*.

Set, O Lord, O *set* apace,
That we may grow from grace to grace;
Till towards the *chace* we nearer draw
The two strong tables of thy law;
Of which the two firm *crosses* be,

The love of man, next after Thee.
The *head sticks* are thy majesty,
The *foot sticks* Christ's humility;
The supplication of the saints,
The *side sticks*, when our faith e'er faints:
Let the *quoins* be thy sure election,
Which admits of no rejection;
With which our souls being join'd about,
Not the least grace can then drop out.
Thy mercies and allurements all,
Thy *shooting stick* and *mallet* call.

But when all this is done we see,
Who shall the *corrector* be?
O Lord, what thou *set'st* can't be ill,
It needs then no *corrector's* skill.

Now, though these graces are all *set*,
Our hearts are but *white paper* yet;
And by Adam's first transgression,
Fit only for the worst impression.
Thy holy Spirit the *pressman* make,
From whom we may perfection take;
And let him no time defer,
To print us on thy character.

Let the ink be black as jet,
What though? it is comely yet
As curtains of King Solomon,
Or Kedar's tents to look upon.

Be victory the *press's head*,
That o'er oppression it may tread:
Let divine contemplation be
The *skrews*, to raise us up to Thee:
The press's *two cheeks* (unsubdued)
Strong constancy and fortitude:
Our slavish flesh let be the *till*,
Whereon to lay what trash you will:
The *nut* and *spindle*, gentleness,
To move the work with easiness:
The *platten* is affliction,

• • • • • • •

WATSON'S *History of the Art of Printing*, etc.   Edinburgh: 1713.

Century Roman. Nine-point, leaded.

BOOKBINDING IN FRANCE IN THE SIXTEENTH CENTURY.

From Italy the art of bookbinding passed into France, where it was brought, during the sixteenth century, to perhaps its greatest perfection. The expeditions of Charles VIII. and Louis XII. into Italy had an important influence upon French art: among other things they were the means of imbuing Frenchmen with an appreciation for Italian bindings. The old heavy covers began gradually to go out of fashion. Almost the last specimen is a velvet binding of a *Book of Hours* inclosed in an iron case of perforated scroll work. The imitation of the Italian style of binding in France gave way to more original attempts towards the end of Francis I.'s reign. Nearly all the bindings of that monarch's time which have come down to us are reproductions of Italian designs and ornamentation generally. In fact, the French school of binding owed its rise entirely to the teachings of Italy, and it was only after a long period of blind subservience that the pupils learned to surpass their teachers. This is clearly seen in the case of Grolier, whose patterns, in spite of their surprising variety, can nearly all be traced back to the designs of Maioli, or Aldo Manuzio, or other Italians. Jean Grolier de Servin, Vicomte d'Aiguisy, the founder of the French

Solid.

school of ornamental binding, and one of the most eminent book collectors of any age, was born at Lyons in 1479. He was descended from an Italian family, and long residence in Italy matured his artistic inclinations. In especial, he cultivated the acquaintance of the celebrated printers—the family of Aldus, of Budæus, Coclius, Rhodiginus, and Erasmus. Louis XII. sent him to Milan as financial administrator, and war treasurer, and he remained there under Francis I. as military commander. Thence he went as ambassador to Rome, and upon his return to France, in 1535, was one of the four Treasurers of the government—an office which he continued to hold during the successive reigns of Francis I., Henry II., Francis II., and Charles IX. He died on the 22d of October, 1565, aged eighty-six. His epitaph at Saint Germain des Prés says less of his honours than of his love and encouragement of letters. The principal occupation of his life was the collection of books, and a large number of contemporary works dedicated to him by both Italian and French authors show the value that was set upon his approval. Gaffori dedicated to him his work on music, printed at Milan in 1518, and in it terms him «*Eminens musarum cultor.*» In 1517, a book on Greek literature, as well as the *Lectiones antiquæ* of Rhodiginus, were addressed to Grolier, and the poet Jean Voulté, whose strictures on all authors were severe, and who condemned even Rabelais, had only praise to give to Grolier. Although he knew that good printers were to be had in France, Grolier went to Italy to find better workmen. His employment of Italian bookbinders was more reasonable, as at that time the art had not attained to anything like perfection in France.

Century Roman.   Nine-point, leaded.

FROM THE «FIRST BOOK OF THE MONARCHIE.»

Prudent Saint Paul doth make narration,
Touching the diverse Needes of every land,
Saying there have been more edification
In five words, that folk do understand,
Then to pronounce of words ten thousand,
In strange language, and knows not what it means;
I think such prattling is not worth two praens.

I would that Prelates and Doctors of the Law,
With Laicke people were not discontent,
Though we into our vulgar tongue did knaw,
Of Christ Jesus the Law and Testament.
And how that we should keep commandement,
But in our language let us pray and read,
Our Pater Noster, Ave, and our Creed.

I would some Prince of great discretion,
In vulgar language plainly causde translate
The needful Lawes of this Region:
Then would there not be halfe so great debate
Among us people of the low estate.
If every man the verity did knaw,
We needed not to treat these men of Law.
        .   .   .   .

Let Doctors write their curious questions,
And arguments sown full of sophistrie:
Their Logick, and their high opinions,
Their dark judgements of Astronomie,
Their Medicine and their Philosophie,
Let Poets shew their glorious engine,
As ever they please, in Greek or in Latine.

But let us have the books necessare,
To Common-wealth, and our Salvation:
Justly translated in our tongue vulgare,
And eke I make you supplication,
O gentle Reader, have none indignation,
Thinking to meddle with so high matter,
Now to my purpose forward will I fare.

Century Roman. Ten-point, leaded.

BOOKBINDING IN THE EIGHTEENTH CENTURY.

In the eighteenth century there were more amateur collectors in France than good binders. Three of them are well known as bibliophilists, and conspicuous among them was the Duke de la Vallière. He was perfectly reckless in his expenditure for books. He spent enormous sums for the possession of rare volumes, and frequented every sale, from which books would be brought in armfuls the next day to his house. In 1771, he bought up the whole of Bonnemet's library for 20,000 livres. His library was estimated by the Swede Liden to contain 30,000 volumes, « all bound in gilt morocco.» When, in 1784, the library was sold, it contained nearly thrice as many books, and was divided into two parts: one of these was composed of 5,668 volumes, catalogued by De Bure, and sold for 464,677 livres; the other half, comprising 27,000 volumes, was bought by M. de Paulmy, and added to his own library, which, being afterwards purchased by the Count d'Artois, became the foundation of the Arsenal Library. M. Girardot

Solid.

was another collector. Liden estimated his library almost more highly than that of M. de la Vallière. He writes: « I have been utterly amazed to meet with such a private collection. It consists almost entirely of rare books; more than you would find in a hundred other libraries. The proprietor is an enthusiast. All the books are bound in gilded morocco.» This collection was the second made by M. de Girardot, the first having been sold to pay his creditors, in 1757. Upon the books of his first collection he had his name stamped in gilt letters, but in those of the second he had a piece of morocco fastened upon the inside of the cover with this inscription: « Ex musæo Pauli Girardot de Préfond.» This collection he also parted with for the payment of his debts. It was bought by Count de Macarthy for 50,000 livres, and placed by him in his own library, which was sold, in 1817, for over £16,000. The third celebrated collector was Gaignat, who possessed a fine library of unique volumes. He had a catalogue made during his lifetime, and left special directions in his will for the sale of his books. But for this proviso, the Empress Catherine would have bought the entire collection. This rage for books extended, in France, even to women.

Century Roman. Ten-point, leaded.

THE EARLY ENGLISH POETS.

See the fathers of verse,
In their rough uncouth dress,
   Old Chaucer and Gower array'd;
And that fairy-led muse,
Which in Spenser we lose,
   By fashion's false power bewray'd.

In Shakspeare we trace
All nature's full grace,
   Beyond it his touches admire;
And in Fletcher we view
Whate'er fancy could do,
   By Beaumont's correcting its fire.

Here's rare surly Ben,
Whose more learned pen
   Gave laws to the stage and the pit;
Here's Milton can boast
His *Paradise Lost;*
   And Cowley his virtue and wit.

Next Butler, who paints
The zeal-gifted saints;
   And Waller's politeness and ease;
Then Dryden, whose lays
Deserv'd his own bays,
   And, labour'd or negligent, please.

There sportively Prior
Sweeps o'er the whole lyre,
   With fingers and fancy divine;
While Addison's muse
Does each virtue infuse,
   Clear, chaste, and correct, in each line.

     .   .   .   .